THE LONELY RICH GIRL

A ROMANCE ALONE NOVEL

© 2017 Urquhart Randolph

VISIT US

WWW.GLOFTON.COM
Enroll in our VIP list.
Be the first to be notified on our latest published book.
Downloading for free gifts.

Disclaimer

This is a work of fiction. Names, characters, organizations, spots, occasions and occurrences are either the results of the creator's creative energy or utilized as a part of an invented way. Any similarity to real people, living or dead, or genuine occasions is absolutely adventitious.

ISBN: 1946792047
eBook: 978-1-946792-24-2
print:978-1-946792-25-9
audio/d :978-1-946792-26-6

Table Of Contents

THE JOURNEY TO LONELINESS

CHAPTER 1

My name is Juan Moore, the second and last child of my parents – Mr. Alfred Moore and Mrs. Marilyn Moore. When I was a kid, my family was just a middle-class family. We weren't wealthy though, but my parents had a decent income. When I was eleven, my family suddenly began the financial rollercoaster drive.

My dad hit a thirty-million-dollar jackpot and since then, there had been no turning back. He and mom quit their banking jobs, invested heavily in the stock markets and they took the bold step of establishing the Moore's Investment Company, which by far, was the most impressive of many decisions they made.

It was a very giant leap for us as family. As a matter of fact, I'd been overwhelmed, impressed, astonished and I must say that pride began creeping sneakily into my heart. I had become the envy of every girl's eye and how guys would have loved just to worship my beauty – Wealth had really brought out the beauty in me.

We relocated to from Colorado to Minnesota. Many a time, my big brother would take me shopping in the classiest malls, visit five star hotels and tourist sites, meet rich guys and families etc. I really loved it. However, my story got a little twisted as the years passed by.

My big brother, Mark, graduated from college when I was fifteen and became the operations manager at the Moore's Investment Company Ltd. Since then, he became as busy as mom and dad. All they ever did was to chase money. All they cared for was to make more money, accumulate cash and swell the wealth. Stupidly enough, my arrogance had driven my old and true friends away.

Now that my mom, dad and brother were all caught up in the same nest, they paid very little attention to me. Money was never a problem but I needed attention and company from my family.

I had already grown fed up with shopping, going to the movies, and having so much fun around. Besides, my brother wasn't going with me anymore. Whenever I was alone on my bed, I realized just how lonely I'd become. There was no more of mummy's goodnight wishes, big brother was so distant and daddy was the worst culprit – paying almost no attention to me whatsoever.

They had the chance to chat at work but when they got home, they were so exhausted that there was little room for family chat. Unfairly, I'd been affected most and sometimes I wished we never ever got wealthy.

At seventeen nearing eighteen, I'd become emotionally very fragile, empty and really needed someone to fill that void. In the past, many people had tried befriending me on social media, from my neighborhood and at high school but I always believed I was too smart for that, thinking they all wanted me as friend for benefits.

Of course, I was the daughter of a millionaire and of a high social class. Well, there were other rich guys that stood up to the occasion and some even dared asking me out but I just wasn't interested. I enjoyed looking tough and independent and besides, most of the rich guys were playboys and a heartbreak was the last thing I needed.

Mark had made a new friend, Anthony Kane. He and his family had recently settled in Minnesota and their paths crossed during a football game where they happened to be passionate fans of the same team, Minnesota Timberwolves.

I could tell from the posts, pictures and activities from Mark's Facebook page and Twitter account that he and my brother had gotten really fond of each other. However, since Mark hardly ever stayed home, he hardly ever brought any friend home. I'd never met Anthony either, but I'd seen his pics and followed him on social media.

Unfortunately, Mark's relentless commitment towards work without taking a leave had taken its toll on him. He got a little sick on one weekend. The family doctor, after diagnosing it was stress-related, recommended that he took a few days off work.

I was glad to hear the news though. At long last, in a long while, I was gonna feel like I had a brother real brother once again. On the Monday, he didn't go to work and I really enjoyed his company. We watched movies, played and laughed all day. I really wished and hoped that that would be a regular thing.

Around 3pm, there was a car horning from the front of our gate. That certainly sounded like none of my family's fleet of cars. I looked through a window and saw a flashy white Nissan Rogue standing behind the gate. The security man, after some minutes of chat with whoever it was, let him in the compound.

The driver got down and after catching a good glimpse of the face, I noticed it was Anthony. Mark, by then, knew it was him and was already in an extra ecstatic mood. I wasn't really happy about his friend coming here. I guess I was just jealous and pissed that I was having a beautiful day with my bro and he'd come to interfere. I went into my room, wore my headset, switched on my IPod, scrolled to my favorite playlist and lay face-up on my bed. After some minutes, I received a text from my brother: Pls come down, Anthony would like to meet you. I chose to ignore it.

Moments later, probably about half an hour, I heard a tap on my shoulder. I opened my eyes and unbelievably, Anthony was standing right beside my bed. How did I not hear nor see him come in? Did he not knock on my door? What kind of a person would just walk into my room like that? Well, I was loving the music so much that I had shut my eyes and was singing passionately to the tunes. That's definitely how come I didn't notice him enter.

CHAPTER 2

I was jittery at the sight of him. I took the headphones off spontaneously and sat up quickly. I avoided eye contact but he stood there, staring at me with a broad smile on his face.

'Hi Juan', he said.

I was quite bemused and yet so pissed. I refused to reply, yet he continued to speak to me.

'I'm sorry if I offended you. I'm Anthony Kane, friend of your brother.'

'I guess that supposes you could bump into my room just like that, right?' I said with a partial frown on my face.

'No dear, I'm sorry. I'd actually been knocking at your door but I guess you couldn't hear me so I called Mark. He climbed up, opened your door and quickly rushed downstairs to continue the movie he's watching.'

'Really, so he did?'

'Yes please', he said with an innocent but charming smile.

'Okay, but it's not okay.'

'May I at least have a seat?' he asked.

'Okay', I said.

I expected he would sit on the chair next to my bed but he sat right beside me on my bed. I drifted further away from where he sat.

'You were singing beautifully. You're such a good singer; great talent.'

'You think so?' I asked.

'Of course, I was really enjoying it and almost didn't want to interrupt'.

'Excuse me!' I said with a shock on my face, 'How long did you say you'd been standing at the door?'

'Actually, I didn't hear much from behind the door but when I entered, I stood beside your bed for probably three or so minutes before tapping your shoulders.'

'Huh!' I exclaimed, burying my face into my pillow for a few minutes.

'Oh no, you were actually great. Don't blame me for not wanting to interrupt a melodious singing session.'

'Alright! Alright! Enough of the flattery okay. When are you going downstairs? My brother must be waiting for you.'

'Seriously? I just got here and you want me to leave already?'

'Well, not exactly but you're the first guy ever to enter my room, you're not just here but also sitting right next to me on my bed and I guess you understand how that makes me feel? Maybe I'll join you guys downstairs later.'

'Okay, sorry but is that why your heart's racing?' He said.

'Excuse me?'

'Never mind. Before I leave, I checked up on your Facebook profile and I realize your birthday is four days from now. Can I take you out for a date?'

'No' I rebutted instantly.

Anthony was a perseverant and very insistent person. He didn't accept that answer without a fight.

'I'm not taking no for an answer because as far as I'm concerned, Mark's told me that you have no boyfriend and there's actually no plan for a birthday party so if you can give me a good reason, then maybe I'd take no for an answer.'

'Well, I have my own plans for my birthday. I want to spend it with family.'

'Really? Family only? So no room for me?'

'I guess so.'

'Alright, as you wish. But you don't have to like me before you know me, you should know me before you hate me.'

I was quite lost as to what he was trying to imply so I asked, 'What are you trying to say?'

He chuckled and said, 'We may not have met in the most glamorous of ways, but don't let that prevent you from getting to know me. I think I like you already.'

'Okay, copy that.'

'Can you at least escort me downstairs?' he asked.

I bluntly repudiated but he stubbornly refused to leave until I accompanied him downstairs. I walked him halfway through the stairs, returned to my room and locked the door.

THE DAWN OF POSSIBLE COMPANIONSHIP

CHAPTER 3

Three days passed by so swiftly. My much awaited birthday was just a day away and I really had great expectations for my birthday. On this day, mom and dad arrived home in the afternoon.

I was happy they did but contrary to my thoughts that they came earlier so we could talk about my birthday, they brought me a reverse news rather.

They'd an urgent business meeting the next day and had to fly to Florida right away. They picked a few personal effects, wished me a happy birthday in advance and set off. I was so furious and mad at them that they couldn't postpone a meeting to spend time with me on my birthday. Even though I was so pissed, they hardly recognized my need for attention.

I was hurt and felt like I really hated them all. It seemed to me that truly, I'd lost my family and probably I needed to find a replacement. I was just in need of someone who could be family to me. Who could be there for me always and willing to hear me out. After they set off, I went into my room, switched off my cell phone, sunk my head into the pillow and wept.

Big bro returned after 7pm. By then, I was still lying in bed. He knocked on my door and I let him. He told me he came home along with Anthony Kane, that he was seated in the living room and would like to see me.

I went to the bathroom to wash down while my brother attended to his friend. I joined them later, after washing down. I was still a little moody when I joined them and I found out he was gonna sleep over but somehow, we spent some really good time together. Anthony was very interesting and jovial. He managed to pull me out of the strong grip of moodiness.

I was seated between both of them on the same couch. The TV was on but he chatted so well, gave us a good treat of jokes that all our focus was on him. By 10pm, big bro had already had enough for the day and was struggling to contain a sleepy head. He stood up and bid as goodnight as he took the lead to go sleep.

Just the two of us were left on the sofa. I'd slept so much during the day and so wasn't sleepy. Anthony wasn't sleepy either. By then, I had already begun to believe I liked him. As we sat together, we talked about our favorite movies and shows, how good I could sing and a number private life issues.

I had my head resting gently on his shoulders, he'd taken my left hand with his right hand and was gently stroking my arms with his palms. It was such a nice feeling and it felt like it'd been ages since someone did that to me – dad and mom used to do it but not anymore.

We'd been quiet for quite a while though he was still cuddling me. Then he called my name gently, 'Juan'.

'Hello' I replied.

'May I ask a question?' He said in a soft voice.

'I'm all ears.'

'You'll turn eighteen in an hour's time. Do you have a boyfriend?'

'Oh' I said in a shy voice, 'I thought you said my bro had told you?'

'Oh yea, he did but I've to hear from the horse's own mouth. Besides he said he wasn't sure.'

'Okay' I said, 'actually I don't have one.'

'Okay. Is there a reason?'

'Not really. Maybe it's just because I feel like I've not met the right person yet or I just feel like I don't really need one.'

'Okay.'

'Why do you ask?' I asked anxiously.

'Why do I ask? You want to know?'

'Yea' I replied excitedly.

'Well, I'm not sure I can explain with words. I may have to demonstrate it.'

'Really? Okay, do so.'

'You're sure I should? You'd have to shut your eyes before.'

I sat up straight and replied anxiously, 'Okay, they're shut!'

I closed my eyes and suddenly, I felt his forehead touch mine. I opened my eyes instantly and my heart began to race rapidly. He was staring straight into my eyes and smiling. I was so nervous and couldn't look him in the eye.

'May I?' He asked, but there was no response from my end. I was so nervous and scared.

'I suppose silence means consent' He said, but once again I could say nothing.

I was still speechless. He withdrew his forehead from mine, placed a kiss on my forehead and smiled again. I had a silly look on my face.

'It's late. Let me walk you to your room.'

I nodded to that, he accompanied me to the front of my door, hugged me affectionately and kissed me again on the forehead.

I lay on my bed for hours but couldn't catch any sleep. I couldn't let him out of my head either. I went on Facebook and as I scrolled through his pics, I beamed with smiles all over. I smiled whenever I recalled the moment when he almost kissed me. Oh, how I would have loved it – my first ever kiss – but I was so nervous at the time.

CHAPTER 4

We were standing on the shores of a very beautiful beach, holding hands and facing each other, He asked if he could kiss me. I nodded excitedly and then without delay, he planted a kiss on my lips. His lips felt so warm. I instantly loosed my lips to accommodate his. It was awesomely sweet.

I was all soaked up in it and just when it was beginning to feel even more sweeter, I could hear the irritating sound of the alarm beeping incessantly. What could my alarm clock be doing with me at a beach? Then I rode out of wonderland, my real eyes flashed open and I saw my hands were clinging on to my bedspread, not Anthony's hands.

Mine 'o' mine, I couldn't believe that it was all a dream. It seemed and felt so real. I had a silly look on my face as I sat on the bed and was just mad at myself that it was all a dream. I really would have relished experiencing that in real life.

I sunk beneath my bed covers, shut my eyes and hoped that the sequel of the dream would manifest but since it naturally wouldn't, I created artificial dreams albeit daydreaming about Anthony. Just a few moments later, my phone began to beep. It was my big bro calling. When I did answer, he sang a happy birthday song for me and by then I realized how I'd almost forgotten it was my birthday.

I was amazed how I could have forgotten it was my birthday because I was so excited about a dream I had. He explained why he had to leave for work so early and because he didn't want to disturb my sleep, he couldn't wish me a happy birthday. He was calling to do just that.

He'd actually left without Anthony and asked him to keep me company till he returned. Prior to calling me, he had called Anthony moments earlier but Anthony told him I hadn't come out of my room yet.

The call was over and I was excited about the fact that Anthony was still in my home albeit a little nervous. I barely knew him, yet it felt like I'd known him in a very long time. Just a few minutes after the call, Anthony knocked on my door.

'Juan, are you there?'

'Yes, I am.'

'When are you coming out or better still can I come in?' He asked.

'No! Actually, I woke up not too long ago. I have to freshen up first. Let me do just that and I'll come see you, okay?'

'Okay dear, I'll be waiting then.'

I rushed quickly and excitedly to the bathroom, freshened up, put on one of my finest clothing, and did my facial makeup. I opened my door and headed downstairs, hoping to meet him at the hall but he wasn't there. I guessed he might be at the kitchen and my guess was right.

As I entered the kitchen, I saw him chatting happily with the house help and she herself was as excited as him. They appeared to be standing too close to each other. I became very jealous and was mad at the maid but couldn't let my feelings out.

'Hey, you're here now. You look gorgeous. Hope you had a good night?'

I nodded with a smile.

'I'm so happy for you today. You're eighteen and a big girl now. I'm gonna sing for you.'

He had gradually managed to draw away from the maid, who was looking on with a broad smile, and began to sing. Oh! He had such an awkward voice and he sang so badly. Though he was very handsome, his handsomeness and his voice were unbelievably so polarized.

I thanked him though when he was done. The house help also joined in the conversation. She too sang me a birthday song and had already prepared something for breakfast so Abraham and I sat at the table and dined together.

He told me he already had my day planned out and that he was gonna take me out. All he needed was my consent. Considering all that love in the air, although he'd not told me the actual details of his plans, I accepted his request.

To my disappointment, he said he was leaving right after breakfast but would return at 2pm to pick me up. I wished he wouldn't have to leave but I couldn't tell him because I didn't want to look emotionally weak in his eyes.

I watched him through the window as he drove away. From my eyes, tears prickled down. I was so sad that he was leaving, yet I was gladdened by the fact that he would return later in the day.

CHAPTER 5

I had donned my elegant sea blue dress and was already in the waiting. Anthony arrived twenty minutes before 2pm.

Before we set off, we spent a couple of minutes together and shared a glass of wine. All along, I was anxious and hopeful that he would pause for a moment and kiss me – as was in the dream – but my expectations didn't materialize.I guess that was a side effect of the dream.

At exactly 2pm, we set off in his car. I had no idea where we were headed since he refused to say. However, wherever we would end up being wasn't much of a concern to me. As long as I was getting to spend the day with him, it was just fine by me.

Anthony drove us to a McDonald's restaurant where we ordered some pizza and fruit juice. He was so boring and quiet but once we got to the restaurant, he spoke a lot and gave me so much to laugh about. He never ceased to amaze me. He actually made a waitress sing a birthday song for me and a thousand eyes turned their attention towards us. It was such an amazing feeling for me.

Having satisfied the ever-present demands of our tummies, he drove us through town at the topmost of speeds, the music so loud, my pretty voice and his awkward one passionately chorusing the lyrics through the music until he pulled the breaks, quenched the music and turned off the ignition. We were right in the center of Mall of America's car park.

As we got down the car, he wrapped his right arms around my waist, headed for the entrance and after some moments of relentless aggressive shopping, we had our shopping baskets full of goodies ranging from clothing to electronic gadgets. I had been to the mall many times but Anthony really made it worth my while. It felt much better and interesting than any shopping I had gone with my big bro, dad, or mom. Perhaps too much love was getting to my head.

With the help of a mall attendant, we carried our goodies into the trunk of the car. We sat in the car. I put on my seat belt but he didn't. He reached out for my seat belt and untucked it from its socket.

I wondered what he was trying to do. He moved closer, his head neared mine, our foreheads kissed and our noses touched each other. With a broad suspicious smile on his face, he began stroking his nose against mine.

Scenes from the dream began flashing back in my mind. I became very anxious as well as nervous. I'd never kissed before. Did I know him well enough to make such commitment? I shut my eyes for a moment and then suddenly, I felt his warm lips touch mine. My heart pounded instantly, then I parted my closed lips. My lower lip was sandwiched between his upper and lower lips. He sucked on it desperately like a piece of candy and I couldn't stop myself from moaning.

I felt a strong sexual sensation rise within me. We kept kissing. My emotions heightened so much and I felt I had become sexually vulnerable. I couldn't control myself anymore. My moans picked up more and more momentum.

He touched my clad cleavage and caused an instant exponential surge in my libido. He touched them softly, then moderately, then begun to squeeze firmly.

It was so sweet that I couldn't bear it anymore. I stopped him. He sat uprightly in his driving seat, and was beaming with smiles all over. I stared at him from the corner of my eyes, still trying to recover from the effect of the ecstatic sexual arousal. He looked at me but I looked away. I was feeling a mix of happiness, shyness and embarrassment.

'You never kissed before?' he asked mockingly.

'Don't start Anthony. Can you please drive?'

He chuckled and said, 'Well, we'll talk about that some other time.'

He ignited the engine, we set off once again without knowing where next he was taking me. I wished up next was home but didn't want to voice it out. We drove through town. He was speeding so fast with the music loudly turned on.

All of a sudden, with a lapse in concentration, he steered into the opposite lane and into the path of an ensuing vehicle. I shrieked.

He turned the steering wheel and applied the brakes. The tires screeched, we hit a bin, the car stopped, and we escaped the approaching vehicle by a hair's breadth.

The engine was off as well as the loud music. My heart pounded. We all had been struck mute by the recent drama. Just when I was beginning to think we have been very fortunate, Anthony said we'd knocked someone down.

He opened the door quickly and rushed out. My heart thumped. I gasped for more air, loosened my seat belt, opened the door and run towards the rear of the car. Truly, we'd knocked someone down. An old grey headed man had already bent over him and was checking his pulse. Shocked, scared and confused, Anthony and I stood by and watched on.

One of the many disgusted visitors screamed, 'You silly driver! Don't just stand there and watch. Call in an ambulance!'

After some moments, the old man said, 'He's got a pulse. He's unconscious, no signs of bleeding yet but there could be internal bleeding.'

We'd already called for an ambulance and in a few minutes, a team of paramedics arrived. The cops followed. The paramedic team attended to the injured man, put him on a stretcher, fitted an oxygen dispensing tube on him, and stretchered him into the ambulance while the police briefly interrogated Anthony and a few of the witnesses. The paramedics briefly examined us, made us lock the vehicle, and took us aboard the ambulance.

We got to Saint Cloud Hospital. We were examined by a team of medics while the injured man was taken to the emergency ward. The medics said we were alright. We'd been waiting for half an hour yet, we had no idea the state of the victim. I had called Mark and let him in on all that had transpired. He was already headed towards us. Before he arrived at the hospital, the police took Anthony away so he could make an official police report and write out a statement. However, I couldn't leave with him. I had to stay behind, just in case something or someone was needed.

My brother arrived a few minutes after 6pm. I was so sad, scared, and really needed him at that point in time. A few moments after he'd arrived, the doctor called for us.

CHAPTER 6

Dr. Benson, as he was called, met us with a smile as we entered his office. He told us the victim had been attended to, that there was a little internal bleeding but his condition was stabilizing and he'd regained consciousness. The news brought so much gladness to our hearts. A nurse led us to the patient's ward so we could see him.

He was asleep when we got there. Big bro suggested he'd go check up on Anthony at the Police Station. Meanwhile, I stayed behind at the hospital, called and made a delivery order for two from McDonalds.

By 8pm, my big bro was on his way back to the hospital. The patient was done with the plate of fried potato chips and chicken I offered him and we were already chatting. I couldn't eat mine because I'd actually lost my appetite. He said his name was Jason Banks and was a twenty-year old waiter at a local restaurant.

I told him how sorry I was about the accident and asked that he forgave us. All my efforts to persuade him into calling his family and informing them were futile. He maintained that he had no family. Big brother and Anthony returned to the hospital around 8:15pm. They also had a short chat with Jason before we left for the house.

I barely said a word on our return home. Mom and dad had heard of the incident and would be making their return the following morning. Upon reaching home, I walked straight into my room without saying a word to anyone. I was mad at everyone for successfully ruining my birthday. I locked the door behind me, stripped off my sweat-drenched dress and went straight into the bathroom to wash down.

As I lay on my bed, I just couldn't cast the thought of Jason Banks out of my head. I couldn't imagine how I would have felt if he had died and though he didn't, I still feared there could be possible health complications for him. I was so mad at Anthony because though he almost ended someone's life, he didn't feel much sympathy or guilt. While returning, he had just been talking about it as a mere misfortune and was more concerned about the state of his Range Rover than the health of the innocent person whose life he'd endangered.

I was seated by Jason on his hospital bed and we were having a nice moment together. He seemed fine and was due to be discharged. While we waited on the doctor's report, Jason suddenly choked on something and began gasping incessantly for breath. I was gripped by a sudden fear. I screamed for help.

The doctor and two nurses rushed in. I was ushered out of the room and looked on from the outside while they attended to him. The doctor shook his head, the nurses pulled a white cloth over his entire body. I knew exactly what that meant. I cried bitterly and uncontrollably, only to wake up and realize that it was all a nightmare. I checked the time and it was 4am. I couldn't sleep again.

By 7:30am in the morning, the maid was done with breakfast. After breakfast, Mark drove me to the hospital but Anthony didn't come along. He said there were some other urgent issues that he needed to attend to so he left in one of my parents' vehicles.

We reached the hospital. Jason was looking much better than he was the previous night. Mark stayed with us about an hour before leaving for work. I stayed with Jason and we had a lengthy chat, trying to get to know each other well.

By 12pm, my parents had returned from Florida and they came to the hospital. They spoke with the doctor and were assured that everything was going to be okay with Jason. There was however a little complication. The doctor said Jason would need to use a wheelchair for about five to six weeks.

When Jason heard the news, he burst into uncontrollable tears. Though the doctor assured him he would be okay, he feared that it could be permanent. I felt so much remorse as I beheld his sad countenance. I could feel his grief. I couldn't just stand there and watch. I walked towards his bed, sat by him, wrapped my hands around his neck and tried my possible best to console him.

By 2pm, the doctor and a nurse returned with an electronic wheelchair for Jason. He got out of the bed and tried it out. It worked perfectly fine. The doctor said he was due to be discharged later in the evening at 6pm. I wasn't happy about Jason's situation – He lived alone and now that he had to utilize a wheelchair, I feared his life would be as miserable as hell.

Although he was initially unwilling, I convinced him into moving in with us until he had fully recovered and was fit to walk again. He was discharged in the evening at 6:30pm and Mark picked us up.

'Where are we headed?' Mark asked as he put on his seatbelt.

'Home' I said.

'Home? What of Jason? Where do I drop him off'? He asked.

'He's coming with us. I've already discussed that with mom and dad?'

'Oh really? Are you sure?' He asked with a huge surprise on his face.

'Certainly!'

He turned on the ignition and drove us home. We put Jason in one of the unoccupied bedrooms downstairs, next to the one Anthony had been occupying. My parents returned from work later in the night and they weren't the least pleased that I'd decided to bring a stranger home. We had a lengthy argument but at the end, they gave up.

WALLOWING IN EMOTIONAL LIMBO

CHAPTER 7

I woke up at 6am the next morning, brushed my teeth, bathed and moved downstairs. Mom and dad were already up and were working out in our home gym. Mark came out from his room already dressed up and set for work.

I smiled at him and asked, 'Hey Mark, did you sleep well?'

He said with a grim look, 'How can I when there's a complete stranger under my roof.'

I could tell he was still pissed that I lied to him in order to bring Jason home. He walked past me briskly without saying goodbye and set off for work. I was hurt by his attitude but I was determined not to let that ruin my ecstatic mood that morning. I entered the gym to greet my parents. As usual, they asked me to join the party but I wouldn't – I had already freshened up and didn't want to get sweaty.

I walked towards Jason's room and knocked on his door.

'Come in, it's not locked' He said.

He was still lying in bed when I walked in.

'Did I wake you?' I asked.

'Oh no, I've been awake for a while.'

'Oh I see. Hope you had a wonderful night?' I said while sitting by him.

'Of course I did. How about you?'

'Oh it was great' I said.

'You're certain of that?'

'Of course I did, at least there were no nightmares.'

'Okay, great. Last night, I could hear you guys.'

'Oh no. Look I'm sorry about that.'

'No, you don't need to be sorry. I didn't hear a single word. I just know it had something to do with me.'

'Okay Jason, please don't dwell on it. Everything will be fine.'

'I'm okay dear' he said with a broad smile.

'But Jason, you know you have to take your medication. Go freshen up. I'll bring you breakfast soon.'

'Alright dear, I'll do so. Thanks a lot.'

I nodded with a super smile on my face as I walked out.

I joined the maid in the kitchen and though she had prepared breakfast already, I prepared a special one for Jason. I cooked custard and made sandwich for him. After mom and dad were done eating, I set the dining table for him. I went to check up on Jason but he wouldn't eat at the dining table. He wanted to eat in his room.

I asked the maid to bring the breakfast in. I sat next to him on his bed and watched him closely while he ate. He looked much more different after freshening up than before. He looked so good and I wondered how I had not noticed such beauty earlier. He had a very innocent young handsome face yet was well-built with great muscles. He was such a humble and polite person.

Even at the hospital, after he had regained consciousness, I feared he would be mad and rude towards us. Yet, he kept his cool without pointing an accusing finger at either of us.

Midway through his meal, he asked if I had taken breakfast. I hadn't. He wouldn't continue his till I took in something. I went to fetch mine, sat by him and we ate.

Just about when he'd taken in his pills, my cellphone began to ring. It was Anthony. I excused myself, left the room and picked the call. Unlike the previous day, I was no longer mad at him but he was. He said he had heard I brought Jason home and questioned my decision to do so. He said awful things that hurt and pissed me off. I dropped the call, went into my room and wept, leaving Jason all by himself.

Some hours later, around 11:00am, Anthony was at my door. I let him in and he came to sit by me. He realized I was sad and hurt so he apologized for the negative things he had said though he still maintained that I shouldn't have brought Jason home.

However, I stood by my decision. To calm the waters, we had a mutual agreement not to talk about it. For a while, none of us had said a word. He kissed me, smiled, and kissed me again. He kissed much more passionately, then I kissed back. Suddenly, I felt like all the anger and hurt had varnished. My sexual drive was already on the ascendency.

He lay me on my back and bent over me, his knees at either side of my waist, then he begun to loosen my shirt's buttons. He loosened all my buttons, and then loosened my bra strap too but I couldn't allow him take them off.

I was shy and nervous. The more I resisted, the more he pressed but I still couldn't let him. He unzipped my jeans. I could not allow him take them off. After so much resistance from my end, he forced his hands through the jeans then my panties but my jeans were just too tight.

He begged to allow him but I just couldn't. He grew increasingly frustrated, got off me and zipped up his flap. I got off the bed, dressed up and fixed my messy hair. I tried explaining to him that I was a virgin, that I wasn't used to that but he was just so pissed was paying no attention to me. He got even more furious when I said we barely knew each other.

'You think I'm a stranger? I guess Jason isn't right?' He burst out.

'No, that's not what I'm implying. I just meant we should slow down and get to know each other more.'

He was already pissed and wasn't gonna have any of what I was saying. He burst out of the room. I chased after him, pleading, but he wouldn't hear me out. He screamed at me to stop following him, stepped out of the house and drove off. I sat on the stairs, buried my face into my hands and wept. A few minutes later, I heard Jason call me. I lifted my head and he was right before me.

'What's wrong dear?' he asked.

I wiped my tears and said, 'It's nothing.'

'Oh come on, I could be of some help. You can talk to me.'

I smiled and said, 'I'm gonna be fine.'

'Okay, I really wish so.'

'Do you mind if I showed you around the house?'

'Oh no, you don't really have to. You know I won't be staying over for long.'

'Even if you won't, I still think I should. I'm really sorry for not returning after I left in the morning. You must have been lonely.'

'No, you don't need to be. I'm cool.'

The maid approached us. Lunch was ready and set on the dining table. We sat at the dining and ate lunch together.

CHAPTER 8

Jason had been with us for five weeks. We'd gotten to know each other very well and he'd been such a great companion.

More awesome was the fact that Jason was such an extremely talented vocalist and had a strong passion for music. We learnt songs together, composed songs and recorded many duets. Unlike me, my family hadn't gotten to know him. They hardly ever spent any quality time with us at home and I knew that they really despised him.

My brother, Mark, despised Jason simply because Anthony never liked him. Anthony had called to apologize for the incident that occurred and we were getting on fine. He hardly came over to the house because he said he hated seeing Jason.

However, Jason and I were doing very great. I had told him my deepest secrets including my experiences with Anthony and I knew his own story and deepest secrets too.

He lost his mom when he was just eleven years old and had to stay with Aunty Mimi, his mom's sister. Mimi was a drug addict and a typical gangster. Jason lived with her and had to endure her unscrupulous attitude and immoral lifestyle until she passed away just when he turned 18yrs old. He became a natural heir to her belongings including her gangster friends. Jason chose to maintain her apartment rather than relocate.

Occasionally, when he was so tight on money, he went to some of his auntie's gangster friends. They made him ran gangster-related errands before they gave him any money. Knowing that he wanted to be nothing like ghetto gangsters, he finally vacated the apartment a year after his auntie's death and traveled to Minnesota to settle down. That's why he had no family and very few friends.

Jason had not been to his place since the accident. He had requested to at least go see his place but I'd always refused. I promised I'd go with him to his place as soon as he could walk again. Fortunately, Jason had begun to walk properly after four weeks. Since I had to honor my promise, I accompanied him to his place. Obviously, there was so much work to be done. He cleaned up the place I made myself useful too.

We returned home afterwards. It was around 9pm when we did. My parents were seated at the hall, eagerly awaiting my return. We greeted them. They queried us. We told them what we'd been up to for the day. I accompanied Jason to his room, returned to my parents and we had a chat. They wanted Jason to leave since he was now fit and they said he would have to do so in two days. I didn't agree but they had made their decision and nothing I said could change that.

My parents left for work the next morning, I knocked on Jason's door and entered so we could chat. We chatted as usual, but it was so difficult to give him the news. He could tell something wasn't right with me. He asked what it was, but I said I was fine. He knew I wasn't and somehow, he figured out what it was.

He sat me down on his bed, held my hands and said, 'I know your family want me to leave but I'm cool with that. You don't have to worry.'

'No, not exactly.'

'Oh come on, I know you want me to stay but try to understand them too. You've gotten to know me, but they still see me as a stranger.'

'But they should get to know you then.' I said with a frustratingly.

He hugged me and said it was gonna be alright. He told me he was gonna leave the next day and I wept. My head was on his laps, sobbing. He continuously cuddled me and consoled me. I wasn't sure anymore what kind of feeling I had for him. Initially, it was sympathy and guilt that made me draw closer but now, we'd become very close, spent a lot of time together, and I feared that probably I was now amorous of him.

'I'm going to be very lonely without you' I said sobbingly.

'No, you'll be just fine. I'll call you always and you have Anthony too.'

'Anthony? I know I love him. I can't deny it, but sometimes I feel like my emotions have clouded my judgment.'

'Why do you say that?'

'Come on Jason, I've been telling you this; he's so secretive and I still don't even know him well. Besides, he hardly talks about things that interest me. It's always been about what he wants.'

'Everything will be just fine, okay?'

'I hope so, I really hope so.'

'Of course it will. There are always gonna be rough times in relationships.'

He prickled me, I laughed as my body reflexed. He did it again and again until I finally got off his lap.

'Okay just stop it' I said, 'I want us to talk, not play.'

'Alright, let's talk then.'

'So when are you getting a girlfriend?' I asked curiously.

'Oh, really?'

'Yea, I would like to know.'

'I don't know. It has to be mutual and she has to be the right person.' He said with a smile.

'Okay. So you've not met the right person yet, I guess.'

'Well, or maybe the right person isn't interested.'

Someone slammed open the door without knocking. We turned in its direction, and there stood Anthony. He stared at us suspiciously.

'Juan, I have to see you.'

'Alright'

I stood up, winked at Jason, told him I'd be back for him and walked after Anthony who was heading towards the hall. As usual, he was pissed to see me with Jason and was always suspicious that something was going on between us. He sat in the sofa and I sat by him.

'Anthony, it's not nice to bump into Jason's room like that. You keep doing it.'

'Well, you owe me a lot of explanations. What had you guys been doing, your hair looks messy?'

'What?'

'Yea, you know what I mean. He's been fucking you, hasn't he?'

'Stop being ridiculous.'

'And stop pretending. You're so fond of him.'

'Please stop, you're hurting my feelings.' I said with tears in my eyes.

'And there we go again. Don't I have feelings too?'

'Why can't you trust me for once?'

'Give me a reason to.' He rebutted.

'Please, let's stop this.'

'No, we're not. You always want to avoid this issue. I just want to know the truth.'

I walked out on him. He pursued me, caught my hands and pulled me back.

'Where do you think you're going? I'm talking to you and you're walking out on me.'

He grabbed me and locked me up tightly in his arms. I wrestled my way out but he wouldn't let go. I screamed, asked him to let go off me but he just wouldn't. Fortunately, Jason came out of his room and to my rescue.

Anthony got pissed and burst into a heated quarrel with Jason. I tried mediating but Anthony slapped me, much to Jason's disdain. He kicked Anthony, pushed him and punched him till he went tumbling to the ground. Anthony's strength was defenseless against Jason's prowess. He lifted himself off the ground, cursed us and went away.

I burst into tears, ran into my room, and locked myself up. Jason followed and knocked that I may let him in but I didn't. I refused to let him in and asked him to leave me alone. After several failed attempts to get me to open the door, he gave up.

Having wept for hours, I got myself off the bed and decided to go see him. As I neared my door, I saw a note had been pushed beneath my door. I picked up the note and it read:

"I really appreciate all the love and support you've shownme but I think I've caused you enough trouble already.

I'm sorry I had to leave this way and I really wish you the best in everything. I'll always have you at heart, Juan."

I didn't want to believe he'd left already –
He said he was gonna leave the next day. I ran
downstairs to his room but he'd already left. I
tried his phone numerous times but there was
no answer.

My family returned much earlier that day
and they were very furious. Anthony had told
them that Jason had assaulted him but when
they arrived, Jason was already gone. They
pointed accusing fingers at me, asked me to cut
my ties with Jason and never see him again. I
disapproved but they were stern and meant
what they said. Frustratingly, I walked out on
them and locked myself up in my room.

CHAPTER 9

I slept every night dreaming about Jason
and wondering what he meant when he said his
dream girl probably did not recognize him. I felt
like a part of me had died away and there was
an emptiness.

The day after he left, we spoke on phone.
He pleaded with me never to come see him, that
he didn't want to be the cause of a family feud
and didn't want to ruin my relationship with
Anthony. He changed his phone number
afterwards.

Two months had passed since Jason left. Anthony and I were still dating but I no longer felt any connection towards him. I'd so many doubts and suspicions about him and he never showed me enough attention.

Whenever I needed Anthony most, he was never available. Whenever he showed up too, he was always bossy and always wanted me to do his bidding without paying attention to whatever my fears and worries were.

Anthony came to see me one evening. Due to previous happenings, I always sat with him at the hall to prevent any sexual temptations. He left around 8pm but unfortunately for him, he left his phone behind. I saw that as a perfect opportunity to prey on his privacy. I went through his WhatsApp chats, emails and other social media messages.

After the things I saw, I was awestruck and brokenhearted. He was a playboy and was part of a WhatsApp group of philanderers who competed among themselves. They posted pics of their victims and mocked how they fell for their tricks. He'd been sending updates on a number of girls he was victimizing and I was no exception.

I wept. I hated myself that the only guy I'd ever kissed was a big time player. Even though we'd never had sex, we had come so close to having sex on two occasions.

I was so broken and needed someone to talk to but there was none. I went downstairs, got out of the house and set off in the Rolls Royce. Minutes after I'd left the house, my parents called but I didn't answer.

They must have noticed that I'd left home. They kept calling till I put off my phone. I had no idea where I was going. I was just riding through town and sobbing until I got to a street. I recognized that was Jason's residence's street. I didn't know what to think but I believed I needed to see him.

I parked the car along the street and walked towards his apartment. It was about 10:30pm. I was about to knock on his door but I feared that perhaps he'd vacated there and there was a new occupant. Nevertheless, I knocked. There was no response. I knocked again and again, but there was still no response. I sat on the floor with my legs bent upward, my knees facing the sky and my hands crossed over my knees. I rested my head on my arms.

I'm not sure how long it was but after a while, someone tapped my shoulders. I rose my head, quickly stood to my feet and wiped the tears off my face with a handkerchief. It was Jason standing before me.

'Juan!' He exclaimed, 'what's wrong?'

I shook my head to mean it was nothing. He slotted his key into the keyhole and opened the door. He let me in, closed the door and locked it up. He was shocked and surprised to see me there.

'Is everything okay?' He asked.

I still wouldn't say a word. He seated me on his sofa, sat by me and I put my head on his laps.

'Can I stay here tonight? Please.' I said.

He stammered, 'W-w-w why? Why do you want to spend the night here?'

I burst into tears again. He cuddled me and tried cheering me up. I'd still not said anything to him. It was getting late yet I hadn't told him what was up. He went to prepare his bedroom, took me there and he returned to the hall. I washed down and put on one of his shirts which reached down to my knee level.

There was no underwear to replace my sweaty panties. I pushed my purse below the pillow but felt a foreign substance beneath it. I checked and they were three pictures of me. I wondered why he would be keeping my pictures beneath his pillow?

I joined him in the hall and sat by him. I looked around. There were a couple of my pictures in frames and a very large one hang on the wall.

'I was expecting you would be sleeping right away.' He said.

'No, I don't feel like it. Not while you're seated over here.'

'Are you willing to talk to me now?' He asked.

'Maybe yes' I said with a faint smile.

'Okay, I'm listening.'

'Why do you have so many of my pictures?' I asked.

He looked amazed by the question.

'Don't be amazed, you have a big one hanging on the wall.'

He chuckled and said, 'Well, I just like them. They're beautiful.'

'That's it?'

'Yes, just that.'

He turned his attention towards the TV and I could tell he had become a little nervous. So many thoughts were rushing through my mind. I wanted to say something but I just didn't know exactly what to say. I turned his face away from the TV and towards me.

I looked straight into his eyes and said, 'Look into my eyes, Jason, and tell me you don't love me.'

He looked awestruck and suddenly went mute. I held his hands and rubbed my thumbs against them, eagerly anticipating his reply but there was none. I drew closer to him and kissed him. He looked into my eyes and smiled shyly. I kissed him again then he kissed back. I laid him on his back, bent over him and we kissed more intimately. I untucked my buttons, he shut his eyes and touched my breasts. I moaned, took off my shirt and opened his flap.

He opened his eyes, caught my hands and halted me in the process. I felt shy and a little embarrassed. I got off him but he stood up and lifted me. I coiled my legs around his waist. He walked us into his room, onto the bed, spread my legs wide open and sweetly deflowered me.

CHAPTER 10

I woke up the next morning feeling so happy. Jason was already awake and was in the shower. I switched my phone on, called my mom and told her about all that I'd discovered on Anthony's phone. She and dad asked me to come home but I refused. I told them I would return after I'd gotten over it. They wanted to know where I was but I never disclosed to them.

Jason came out of the bathroom looking fresh and very handsome. He'd already prepared breakfast for us and wanted to report to work but I didn't want him to. I told him money wasn't a problem, that I had enough money to cater for us but he said he didn't want to feed on my money.

I told him not to go if he really loved. He was reluctant but in the end, he didn't go. We ate breakfast together and afterwards, I told him all that had unfolded. He comforted me and assured me he would never ever hurt me.

I had been with Jason for three days and had managed to get him to quit his job permanently.

I spoke to my parents and informed them that I'd chosen to be with Jason Banks, that they should please accept him but my dad had sworn never to approve that. He said I had to choose between family and Jason because I couldn't belong to both.

My mom and big bro said they wanted what's best for me and beckoned on me to come home but none of them could assure me that they would stand by me and make dad loosen his stance. I decided to ignore all other distractions and concentrate on Jason who I considered as my true family.

Jason made me a promise to fight till he became a better person and to cause my family to rethink their stance. He knew the main reason why they didn't like him was because he didn't have a strong financial status nor high education.

Three months passed by. Anthony, having not repented of his demonism, had been jailed for making and sharing sextapes of innocent girls as well as sexually abusing a number of women. Meanwhile, my bond with Jason grew stronger each day and I had managed to inspire him to follow after his passion, no matter what the challenges were.

His passion had always been music and nothing less. I'd been supporting us with my bank balance and he'd been treating me like a princess. Jason had been working very hard on his music and we were set to record an album.

Finally, we recorded Jason's first album, titled *The Transformed*. It consisted of twelve tracks. It was a huge risk since the budget sunk our finances. We were left with less than a thousand dollars after recording the album and were just on the brink of bankruptcy.

By week three of the album's release, Jason's tracks had already gone viral. Sale of the mp3 and music videos were extremely high. It was amazing how we had already begun earning some money from ITunes, YouTube etc. Jason had a call from his manager. The manager told him he had received his first endorsement proposal worth one million US dollars as well as a fifty-thousand-US-dollar-worth invitation to an entertainment concert which was due in the next three months. It was such a shocking news. He was dumbfounded and reduced to tears.

It had been six months since I left home. Jason and I had already bought a house and were settled in it. He asked me to go back home during the weekend and that he would come see my family.

I went home on a Sunday and met my mom first. She hugged me and we were reduced to tears. Then my big bro and dad also came around. My father had a grim look on his face when I told him I was still gonna be with Jason but he didn't start a fight. I told him Jason would come at 2pm and so he could face him as a man.

Jason came home at 2pm in an SUV. My dad fumed that I'd spent the little money I had on a Jason Banks – the only Bank without a penny. Jason admitted that he had no money and that I had indeed spent all my money on him. He said in so doing, I had made him realize his potential and transformed him into the star he always dreamt of becoming. They had heard of a new musician called Jason Banks, but they never knew it was the Jason Banks that had lived under their roof, neither did they know I was his eighteen-year-old producer.

Jason said to them, 'I knew you hated me because you loved your daughter and wanted the best for her. I wasn't anywhere near good enough. I'm still not good enough yet but better than yesterday. Tomorrow is gonna be better than today and I bare no grudge against you. At least for her sake, let's bury the past and be family.'

My dad admitted he was ashamed of himself, my mom too. They hugged him and Mark embraced me. They gave their consent and tears streamed down my eyes. I walked towards Jason and kissed him before everyone's eyes.

I like to write great romance stories that take you on an emotional journey whether tears, laughter (or both) or just steamy hot fun (or all of them).

Please... leave a review, let me know if you had enjoyed read this great story?

THANK YOU ☺

VISIT US

WWW.GLOFTON.COM
Enroll in our VIP list.
Be the first to be notified on our latest published book.
Downloading for free gifts.

www.ingramcontent.com/pod-product-compliance
Lightning Source LLC
Chambersburg PA
CBHW050911120626
46552CB00004B/1526